The Jungle Book

Rudyard Kipling

Simplified by D K Swan
Illustrated by Alan Marks

Longman

Longman Group UK Limited,
Longman House, Burnt Mill, Harlow,
Essex CM20 2JE, England
and Associated Companies throughout the world.

First published 1991

ISBN 0-582-03587-2

Set in 12/14 point Linotron 202 Versailles
Produced by Longman Group (FE) Limited
Printed in Hong Kong

Acknowledgements

The cover background is a wallpaper design called NUAGE,
courtesy of Osborne and Little plc.

Stage 1: 500 word vocabulary

Please look under *New words* at the back of this book
for explanations of words outside this stage.

Contents

Introduction

Rudyard Kipling

Rudyard Kipling, the writer of these short stories, and of novels and poetry, was born in Bombay in India in 1865. His father sent him to England as a child. At first he lived there with people of his father's family. Perhaps they did not understand the boy from India: Kipling was very unhappy with them.

In 1882, at the age of seventeen, Kipling returned to India. He stayed there for seven years, working for English-language newspapers. While he was doing that, he began to write the short stories that made him famous. They were first printed in India. Then they came out in England in collections like *Plain Tales from the Hills* (1887). They pleased a lot of readers because Kipling understood and liked the unimportant people of the world, people like poor Indian villagers and the ordinary British soldiers – the "privates" – of the army in India.

Some of his novels – longer stories, each filling a book – were good. *Kim* (1901), the exciting story of a British boy in India, is perhaps his best novel. *Stalky & Co.* (1899) does not please everyone. It is a school story, set in the school in

England that Kipling went to, and *The Concise Cambridge History of English Literature* (1941) called it "an unpleasant book about unpleasant boys in an unpleasant school".

Kipling as a writer of poetry was well liked. He could make music of the way of speaking of ordinary people, even the bad English of people with little education.

> It's Tommy[1] this, an' Tommy that, an'
> "Chuck[2] him out, the brute[3]!"
> But it's "Saviour of his country" when the
> guns begin to shoot.

([1] name for any "private" soldier; [2] throw; [3] nasty man)

The best collections of Kipling's poetry are perhaps *Barrack-Room Ballads* (1892) and *The Seven Seas* (1896).

The Jungle Book was printed in 1894. Readers of all ages love it. The same is true of Kipling's *Just So Stories* (1902), another collection of stories; these tell us how the elephant got his trunk, how the rhinoceros got his skin, how the whale got his throat, and other wonderful things. Kipling knew a lot about animals, but in *Just So Stories* and in *The Jungle Book* the animals are people. In *Just So Stories* the elephant's child asks the crocodile to stop pulling his nose – to let him go, because he is hurting him. He sounds very much like a human child whose nose is being pulled: "Led go! You are hurtig be!" In *The Jungle Book* even those dangerous snakes the cobras sound like human mothers when they ask Baloo, Bagheera and Kaa to take seven-year-old Mowgli away: "Take him away. He is so excited that he can't stand still. He'll hurt our young ones. Take him away."

Rudyard Kipling's life ended in a beautiful old house in Sussex in England in 1936. His body lies with the best-known and best-loved writers of English literature in the Poets' Corner in Westminster Abbey in London.

Mowgli's brothers

At seven o'clock on a hot evening in the Seeonee hills, Father Wolf woke up. He looked across the cave at Mother Wolf. She had her four very young cubs beside her; the moonlight came into the cave and showed them to him.

"It's time to hunt again," said Father Wolf. And he was just going to start down the hill when a little animal came to the mouth of the cave.

"Good hunting, Great Wolf," the little animal said. "And I hope your fine children will have strong white teeth, and will hunt well, and will always remember the hungry ones."

It was Tabaqui, the jackal. The wolves of India don't like Tabaqui. He makes trouble, and he goes to the houses of men to find food that they have thrown out. Father Wolf could see from Tabaqui's eyes that he wanted to make trouble now.

"Shere Khan, the Big One, has changed his hunting grounds," Tabaqui said. "He is going to hunt among these hills, he told me."

Shere Khan was the tiger who lived near the Waingunga River, thirty kilometres away.

"He can't do that!" Father Wolf said angrily.

"By the Law of the Jungle he mustn't change his hunting grounds without telling us that he is going to do it. He will frighten away all the animals. And I – I have to kill for two, these days."

"Shere Khan has always had one bad foot," said Mother Wolf quietly. "That is why they call him Lungri, and that is why he kills only the villagers' cattle. Now the villagers of the Waingunga are angry with him, and he has come here to make *our* villagers angry. They will bring fire to the grass, and that will make danger for us and our children."

"You can hear him now," said Tabaqui.

Father Wolf listened. Far down below the cave, he heard the angry cry of a tiger who has caught nothing.

"The fool!" said Father Wolf. "To begin a night's hunting with that noise is very foolish. Does he think that our sambur deer are like his fat Waingunga cattle?"

"H'sh!" said Mother Wolf. "He isn't hunting cattle or deer tonight. He's hunting Man."

"Man!" said Father Wolf. "Ugh! Aren't there any frogs for him to eat?"

By the Law of the Jungle, no animal should kill and eat Man. There is a reason for every law. The real reason for this one is that if a man is killed, other men soon come on elephants, with guns and hundreds of other men who make a great noise. And that is bad for everybody in the jungle. But that isn't the reason that the animals themselves give. They say it isn't right to hurt a thing that can't fight for its life. And they say that man-eaters become sick and lose their teeth.

Suddenly there was a cry – an untigerlike cry – from Shere Khan. Father Wolf ran out of the cave and heard Shere Khan cry out again and fall about in the jungle.

"The fool," said Father Wolf. "He has jumped at a woodcutter's fire and burnt his feet."

"Something is coming up the hill," said Mother Wolf. And she moved one ear. "Be ready."

There was a sound in the grass near the cave. Father Wolf went down on his back legs, ready for his jump. He began his jump, but stopped it in the air.

"Man!" he cried. "A man's cub. Look!"

It was a very young brown child who had learnt to walk only a week or two before – a naked child whose big eyes showed no fear. He looked up at Father Wolf and laughed.

"Is that a man's cub?" said Mother Wolf. "I have never seen one. Bring it here."

A wolf can move his own cubs without hurting them. Father Wolf's white teeth made no mark on the child's naked back as he took him up and put him down among the cubs.

"How little! How naked, and – how brave!" said Mother Wolf softly. The child was pushing his way between the cubs to get near to her. "*Ahai*! He is taking his milk with the others."

Something stopped the moonlight coming into the mouth of the cave: Shere Khan's great head and shoulders were pushed into the opening. Tabaqui, behind him, was excited: "My lord, my lord, it went in here!" he cried.

Father Wolf spoke quietly, but his eyes were angry. "What do you want?" he asked Shere Khan.

"I want my food. A man's cub came here. Its father and mother have run away. Give it to me."

Shere Khan had jumped at a woodcutter's fire, as Father Wolf had said, and he was very angry because his feet were burnt. But Father Wolf knew that the mouth of the cave was too small for a tiger to come through.

"The Wolves are a free people," said Father Wolf. "They take orders from the Head of the Pack, and not from any cattle killer. The man's cub is ours – to kill if we want to."

"If you want to?" The tiger's roar filled the cave with sound. "What do you mean? It is I, Shere Khan, speaking to you!"

Mother Wolf left the cubs and went towards the tiger. "And it is I, Raksha, answering you!" she said. "The man's cub is mine, Lungri – mine! No one will kill him. He will live to run with the Pack, and to hunt with the Pack. And in the end, you hunter of little naked cubs – frog-eater –

4

fish-killer – he will hunt *you*! Now go!"

Shere Khan knew that he was in a bad place, and that Mother Wolf had not been called Raksha, the Dangerous One, for nothing. So he moved back from the cave mouth. And when he was safely away, he shouted, "We'll see what the Pack will say about this caring for man cubs. The cub is mine, and he will come to my teeth in the end!"

Mother Wolf went back to the cubs. Father Wolf said to her, "Shere Khan is right in one thing. We must show the cub to the Pack. Do you still want to keep him?"

"Keep him?" she cried. "He came naked, at night, alone and very hungry, but he was not afraid! Look, he has pushed one of my cubs to one side. And cattle-stealing Lungri wanted to kill him, and then the tiger would have run away to the Waingunga, while the villagers here brought men with guns to hunt us everywhere in these hills. Keep him? Of course I'll keep him. One day Mowgli – I'll call him Mowgli, the Frog – will hunt Shere Khan."

"But what will our Pack say?" said Father Wolf.

The Law of the Jungle is clear: when cubs can stand on their feet, the father must bring them to the Pack meeting at the Council Rock at full moon. The other wolves must see them and know them. After that, the Pack will take care of the cubs, and nobody must hurt them.

Raksha tells Shere Khan that the man's cub is hers

On the night of the next Pack meeting, Father Wolf took his cubs and Mowgli and Mother Wolf to the hilltop Council Rock. The Leader of the Pack at that time was Akela, the great grey wolf. From his place on the highest rock, Akela looked down at the ring of about forty wolves. The cubs played in the centre of the ring.

One after another, a father or mother pushed a cub into the open place below Akela. Then the Leader of the Pack called out, "You know the Law. Look well, Wolves! Look well!"

The wolves looked at cub after cub. Sometimes one of the older wolves went quietly to look carefully at a cub, and then went back to his place on feet that made no sound.

At last Father Wolf pushed "Mowgli the Frog" into the open place. The child sat there, laughing and playing happily with some little round stones that looked pretty in the moonlight.

Akela never moved his head. He called again, "Look well, Wolves! Look well!"

A roar came from outside the ring of wolves – the voice of Shere Khan crying, "The cub is mine. Give him to me. Why do the Free People want a man's cub?"

Akela did not even move his ears. He only said, "Look well, Wolves! Why should the Free People listen to any other people? Look well!"

"That's right," said most of the wolves. But

one young wolf said, as Shere Khan had said, "Why do the Free People want a man's cub?"

The Law of the Jungle is clear: if any wolf questions the right of a cub to become one of the Pack, two who are not the father and mother must speak for that cub.

"Who speaks for this cub?" said Akela. "Among the Free People, who speaks?" There was no answer, and Mother Wolf got ready for a fight. She knew that, if she fought, it would be her last fight.

There is one other, not a wolf, who may speak at Pack meetings. Baloo, the sleepy brown bear, teaches the wolf-cubs the Law of the Jungle, and he can go where he likes. Old Baloo stood up on his back legs and spoke.

"The man's cub?" he said. "I speak for the man's cub. A man's cub hurts nobody. Let him run with the Pack. I myself will teach him."

"We need one other," said Akela. "Baloo has spoken, and he is our teacher for the young cubs. Does any other speak?"

A black shape dropped into the ring of wolves. It was Bagheera the Black Panther. Everybody knows Bagheera, and nobody wanted to quarrel with him, because he is quicker than Tabaqui, braver than any other animal, and very dangerous. But he had a voice as soft as a summer night.

"Akela and all you Free People," he said quietly. "You didn't ask me to come to your meeting, but the Law of the Jungle says: 'If there is a question about a cub, that cub can be bought for a price.' The Law doesn't say who may pay that price. Am I right?"

"Right!" said the young wolves, who are always hungry. "Listen to Bagheera. The cub can be bought for a price. It is the Law. Speak, Bagheera."

The Black Panther said, "There is a bull – a fat one, newly killed – less than a kilometre from here. I am ready to give you that bull if you say that the cub may live and run with the Pack."

There were a lot of voices: "Why not? He'll die in the cold months. Or he'll die in the hot months. How can a naked frog hurt us? He can run with the Pack. Where is the bull, Bagheera?"

And then Akela's voice was heard: "Look well, Wolves! Look well!"

Mowgli didn't stop his game with the pretty little stones. He didn't notice when the wolves came and looked at him, one after another. At last they all went down the hill for the dead bull. Only Akela, Bagheera, Baloo, and Mowgli's own wolves were left at the Council Rock. Shere Khan still roared somewhere in the night. He was very angry that the wolves hadn't given the man-cub to him.

"It was well done," said Akela. "Men and their cubs are wise. Perhaps he will help us one day."

Bagheera and Baloo speak for Mowgli at the Council Rock

"True," said Bagheera, "because t|
won't always have the wisest wolf as its l|

"Take him away," Akela said to Fathe\ ̣ᴗıı,
"and make him learn how to live as one of the
Free People."

And that is how Mowgli became one of the
Seeonee Wolf Pack, at the price of a bull and
with Baloo's word.

Now you must move on for ten or eleven years.
You can't read all about the wonderful times
that Mowgli had with the wolves, because that
would fill very many books. He grew up with
the cubs, and Father Wolf taught him how to
live in the jungle. He learnt the meaning of
every sound in the grass, every change in the
night air, every note of the birds' call, every plop
of a little fish jumping in the water.

When he was not learning, Mowgli sat in the
sun and slept, and ate, and went to sleep again.
When he was dirty or hot, he went into the little
forest rivers. When he wanted honey (Baloo
taught him that honey and nuts are nice to eat),
he climbed up the trees for it. Bagheera showed
him how to do that.

He took his place at the Council Rock when
the Pack met. And there he found that he had a
certain power: if he looked hard at one of the
wolves, that wolf dropped his eyes. At other
times he pulled the long thorns out of the feet of
his friends; wolves have a lot of trouble with

thorns in their feet from the thorny trees and bushes in the forest.

Sometimes Mowgli went down from the hills to the villagers' fields at night. He looked at the villagers in their little houses. But he didn't trust men. Bagheera stopped him more than once from walking into a trap that men had hidden in the jungle.

He grew strong, as a boy must grow when he doesn't know that he is learning any lessons. Mother Wolf told him not to trust Shere Khan. "One day, you must kill him," she said. A young wolf would have remembered that. Mowgli didn't remember it, because he was only a boy.

Shere Khan was often in the same part of the jungle as Mowgli, because Akela was becoming older and not so strong, and so the tiger was making himself the friend of the younger wolves. They followed him for the bits of food that he didn't want. Akela didn't like that, but he was getting too old to stop them. So Shere Khan said, "Why do fine young hunters like you stay in a Pack with a dying leader and a man's cub? They tell me that at the Council Rock you can't look into the man-cub's eyes." And the young wolves were angry and hated Mowgli.

Bagheera knew a little about this. He spoke to Mowgli about it. Mowgli laughed and said, "But I have the Pack, and I have you. And Baloo would fight for me. Why should I be afraid?"

"Open your eyes, Little Brother. Shere Khan

isn't a danger to you in the jungle. But remember that Akela is old now. When he can't kill a deer, he won't be the leader. And most of the wolves who looked at you at the Council Rock are old, too. The young wolves believe – as Shere Khan has told them – that a man-cub ought not to be in the Pack."

Mowgli said, "I have never broken the Law of the Jungle. And I have pulled thorns from the feet of every wolf in the Pack. Surely they are my brothers!"

"Brothers? They will kill you if they can."

"But why? Why do they want to kill me?"

"Look at me," said Bagheera. And Mowgli looked at him between the eyes. The big panther turned his head away. "That is why," he said. "They hate you because their eyes can't meet yours – because – yes, because you have pulled thorns from their feet – because you are a man."

"I didn't know that," said Mowgli.

"You need to know it," his friend said. "Listen. When Akela can't kill a sambur – and that may be soon – the Pack will turn against him, and against you. They will have a meeting at the Council Rock, and then – and then – Ah! I know! This is what you must do. Go down to the village at the foot of the hill, and take some of the Red Flower that they grow there. Then, when the time comes, you will have a stronger friend than Baloo or me or those of the Pack who love you. Get the Red Flower."

Bagheera meant fire. He called it the Red Flower because, like every beast in the jungle, he was afraid of it.

"The Red Flower?" said Mowgli. "It grows outside their houses in little pots. I'll get some."

He started down towards the little river at the foot of the hill. And there he stopped because he heard the sound of the Pack hunting. His ears told him that they were following a big sambur. He heard the big deer turn to fight. Then there were cries from the young wolves: "Akela! Akela! Let the leader show how strong he is! Go in, Akela!"

The sounds told Mowgli that Akela went in alone, that his teeth did not get their hold, that the sambur's kick made him fall.

Mowgli didn't wait. He went on into the village and looked through the window of one of the houses. He saw how they gave food to the fire. He saw a child fill a pot with pieces of the fire and bring it outside. He took the pot from the child.

All the next day, Mowgli learnt about his fire pot.

In the evening, Tabaqui came and told him that he must go to the Council Rock. He laughed, and Tabaqui ran away, frightened. Then Mowgli went to the Council Rock, still laughing.

Akela was by the side of his rock, not on top of it. That meant that another wolf could try to become the Leader of the Pack. Shere Khan, with his following of young wolves, walked openly on the Council Rock.

Mowgli sat down, with the fire pot between his knees. Bagheera came and lay beside him.

Shere Khan began to speak. He would not have been so brave when Akela was younger.

Mowgli jumped up. "Free People," he cried. "Is Shere Khan the Leader of the Pack? Why is he here at all?"

Akela looked up. "Free People – and you, too, jackals of Shere Khan – for many years I led you to and from the kill, and in all that time not one of you has been hurt or caught in a trap. Now I have failed to kill, and so you will be right to kill me here on the Council Rock now. So I ask, who is coming to make an end of Akela? The Law of the Jungle, as you know, says that you must come one at a time."

Nobody spoke. There was not a wolf who would fight Akela alone.

Then Shere Khan roared, "Bah! What do we care about this old fool? He is going to die soon. It is the man-cub who has lived too long. Free People, he was mine from the beginning. Give him to me."

Akela spoke again. "Mowgli has eaten our food. He has lived with us. He has helped us in the hunt. He has always kept the Law of the Jungle."

"He is a man – a man!" cried most of the

wolves angrily, and they moved to where Shere Khan was.

"Now your friends can do nothing more – only fight for you," said Bagheera.

Mowgli stood up, with the fire pot in his hands. "Listen, you!" he cried. "I would have been a wolf with you until I died. But you have told me very clearly that I am a man, and so it must be true. I will not call you my brothers any more, but dogs, as a man should. *You* will not say what is to happen to me: *I* will. And to make this clear to you, I have brought here a little of the Red Flower – the Red Flower you fear."

He threw the fire pot on the ground, and some of the fire fell out. The wolves moved back in great fear as Mowgli put a stick into it and the stick started to burn.

"Good!" said Mowgli. "I can see that I was right: you are dogs. I am going to leave you. I'll be a man among men. But first I must speak to this animal." And he stepped to where Shere Khan sat looking foolishly at the burning stick. Bagheera followed because Mowgli was stepping into danger.

"This cattle killer," Mowgli said, "wanted to kill me here because he failed to kill me when I was a cub. Well, this is how we beat dogs when we are men. If you move, Shere Khan, I'll push the Red Flower into your mouth." He beat Shere Khan on the head with his burning stick, and the tiger cried out in great fear.

Mowgli beats Shere Khan with a burning stick

"Bah!" said Mowgli. "Are you brave now? Go! But you must all know this: the next time I come to the Council Rock, it will be with Shere Khan's skin. And know this, wolves: Akela goes free, to live where he pleases. You will *not* kill him, because that is my order. And I don't think Shere Khan's 'friends' will come here to the Council Rock any more. I must drive you out – like this! Go!" The fire was burning strongly at the end of the stick, and Mowgli hit out with it as the young wolves ran crying with fear.

At last there were only Akela, Bagheera, and perhaps ten wolves that had always loved Mowgli. Then something began to hurt Mowgli inside him, as he had never been hurt before, and the tears ran down his face.

"What is the matter with me?" he said. "Am I dying, Bagheera?"

"No, Little Brother. Those are only tears – men's tears. Now I know you are a man, not a man's cub any more. Don't be afraid of the tears, Mowgli. They are only tears."

So for the first time Mowgli cried.

"Now," he said, "I will go to men. But first I must say goodbye to my mother." And he went to the cave where she lived with Father Wolf, and he cried on her coat.

Daylight was coming when Mowgli went down the hill alone, to meet those unknown things that are called men.

Kaa's hunting

This is a story of the days when Baloo was teaching Mowgli the Law of the Jungle. It was before Mowgli left the Seeonee Wolf Pack.

The big old brown bear Baloo was really glad to have a quick learner like Mowgli. As a man-cub, Mowgli needed to learn much more than a young wolf. The boy could climb quickly, run fast, and swim well. So Baloo taught him how to call to the people of the forest, the land, and the water.

"I am now teaching him the Master Words of the Jungle," Baloo told Bagheera. "Now, Mowgli, say the words for the Hunting People."

"We are brothers, you and I," said Mowgli. He said the words the way all the Hunting People say them.

"Good," said Baloo. "Now the words for the birds."

The answer was ended with the high whistle of Chil, the Kite.

"Now for the Snake People," said Baloo.

"We are brothers, you and I," said Mowgli, with the snake *hiss* that is not like any other sound.

"Now he needn't fear anybody," Baloo said

to Bagheera.

Mowgli laughed. "Not even old Baloo," he said. "I'll go up the trees and throw sticks and dirt down at old Baloo. That's what the *Bandar-log* do. They say *I* can do it, and they'll help me."

"Mowgli," said Baloo, "you have been talking to the *Bandar-log*, the monkeys who live in the trees." His eyes were angry.

Mowgli looked at Bagheera to see if the panther was angry too. Bagheera's eyes were as hard as stones.

"When Baloo hurt my head," said Mowgli, "I went away, and the *Bandar-log* came down from the trees and were kind to me. I hadn't any other friends then."

Baloo was still angry. "Listen, Man-cub!" he said, and his voice was hard. "I have taught you all the Law of the Jungle for all the people of the jungle, but not the *Bandar-log*. They have *no* law. Their way is not our way. They have no leaders. They remember nothing. We People of the Jungle do not take notice of the monkeys. We don't drink where they drink. We don't go where the monkeys go. We don't hunt where they hunt. Have you ever heard me speak of the *Bandar-log* until today?"

"No," said Mowgli, very quietly because the angry Baloo frightened him.

"No," said Baloo. "The Jungle People don't speak about them. There are very many of them, and they are bad, dirty animals. We don't take notice of them, even when they throw things on our heads. Remember that."

While Baloo was speaking, there were monkey people high up in the trees over their heads. They followed Baloo, Bagheera and Mowgli through the jungle very quietly until it was time for the midday sleep. Mowgli, between the panther and the bear, was thinking as he fell asleep, "I'll never think about the *Bandar-log* again."

The next thing he knew was when a lot of hard, strong little hands took hold of him and carried him up into the treetops. Far down on the ground he saw his friends: Baloo waking the jungle with his cries; Bagheera climbing up the tree with every tooth showing.

The *Bandar-log* shouted as they took Mowgli up to the highest parts of the trees, where the panther could not follow. Then they started their journey along the monkey roads, shouting and jumping from tree to tree. For a time, Mowgli was afraid that they would drop him – and in some parts of the monkey road he was thirty metres from the ground – but then he began to think. The first thing was to send word to Baloo and Bagheera because he knew his friends couldn't travel as fast as the monkeys. If he looked down, he could see only the trees. So he looked up, and saw Chil, far away in the blue sky. Chil the Kite rode in the air. His wonderful eyes saw everything in the jungle. He saw that the monkeys were carrying something, and he came down a few hundred metres to see. He whistled in surprise when he saw Mowgli being pulled up to a treetop. He was more surprised still when Mowgli gave the kite call for: "We are brothers, you and I."

The trees hid the boy after that, but Chil rode the air to the next high part of the monkey road. The little brown face came up again. "See where we go!" Mowgli shouted. "See where we go, and tell Baloo of the Seeonee Pack and Bagheera of the Council Rock."

"In whose name, brother?" Chil had never seen Mowgli, but of course he had heard about him.

"Mowgli, the Frog. Man-cub, they call me. See where we go!"

Chil climbed up into the sky until he could hardly be seen. There he used his wonderful eyes, seeing the treetops moving as the monkeys carried Mowgli along.

"Because they live in trees, the *Bandar-log* have no fear of any of our people," Baloo said. "They are afraid of only Kaa the Rock Python. The great snake can climb as well as they can. He steals the young monkeys in the night. His name makes the *Bandar-log* cold with fear. Perhaps he will help us."

Baloo and Bagheera found Kaa lying in the sun. He had changed his skin in the last ten

days, and he was very pleased with his new coat
– the beautiful new brown and yellow coat that
covered the ten metres of his body.

"Good hunting, Kaa!" cried Baloo.

"Oho, Baloo, what are you doing here? Are
you looking for food? I, too, am hungry. Have
you seen any deer?"

"We *are* hunting," said Baloo slowly. He
knew that you must not hurry Kaa. He is too big.

"We are looking for the *Bandar-log*," said
Bagheera. "Those dirt-throwers have stolen
away our Man-cub. Perhaps you know about
him."

Kaa said, "I did hear something about a
man-thing that was in a wolf pack."

"Our Man-cub is in the hands of the *Bandar-
log* now," said Baloo. "We know that they are
afraid only of Kaa among all the jungle people.
And so we have come to you."

"If the man-thing is with them, he is in great
danger," said the python. "Where did they take
him?"

"We don't know," said Baloo very sadly.

"Up! Up! Look up, Baloo of the Seeonee
Pack! Look up!"

Baloo looked up to see where the voice came
from. He saw Chil the Kite coming down out of
the evening sun.

"What is it?" Baloo called.

"I have seen Mowgli among the *Bandar-log*.
He told me to tell you. I saw the *Bandar-log* take

him across the river to the monkey city."

They all knew about the city. Men had left it hundreds of years before, and the jungle had hidden it. The monkeys often went there, but the Hunting People did not. They keep away from places that men have used.

"It's half a night's journey at least," said Bagheera.

"You and Kaa go on," said Baloo. "I'll follow as fast as I can."

Bagheera hurried away at the quick panther run. The great Rock Python went as quickly.

In the old city, the Monkey People were not thinking about Mowgli's friends. They had the boy in the Lost City, and they were very pleased with themselves. Mowgli had never seen a city before. This one was very old and broken. There were no roofs on the tops of the houses. Trees had grown through the old stone walls. But it was wonderful in Mowgli's eyes. The monkeys brought him there late in the afternoon, and then they began to play among the old houses. They ran up and down the old city roads, and threw sticks and stones. They drank at the stone water tanks, and made the water dirty.

"Don't they ever sleep, these *Bandar-log*?" Mowgli wondered. But night came, and they were still playing.

"I want food," Mowgli shouted at them. "I don't know this place, so bring me food. Or

The monkeys take Mowgli to the Lost City

leave me alone, and then I can hunt."

Twenty or thirty monkeys ran to get food from the jungle trees. But they started fighting on the way, and they didn't remember to bring any food.

Every time Mowgli went near the city wall, a lot of the monkeys pulled him back.

"You mustn't leave us," they said. "We are a great people. We are free. We are the most wonderful people in the jungle. We all say that, and so it must be true."

They took him to a building with water tanks round it. It had been a beautiful white building for queens hundreds of years before. There were no doors to the building. The stone roof had fallen in, and the stones from it hid the underground way into it – the way from the king's palace higher up the hill. There were no windows, but the white stone of the walls had thousands of small openings like stars. The building looked beautiful in the moonlight.

The open place in front of the white building was a meeting place for the monkeys. Hundreds of them came and stood round Mowgli. They all told him how wonderful the *Bandar-log* were. "This is true!" they all shouted. "We all say so, so it is true!"

"They never sleep," Mowgli thought. "Now a big cloud is coming to cover the moon. If it's a really big cloud, perhaps I can run away when it stops the moon's light. But I'm very tired."

Two good friends were watching the same cloud. They were just outside the city, but they had stopped there to make a plan. Bagheera and Kaa knew how dangerous the Monkey People are when there are a lot of them. The monkeys only fight when there are a hundred of them against one. Not many of the jungle people like to fight a hundred to one.

"I'll go round to the far side of the city," Kaa said, "and then I'll come down the hill very fast. They won't throw themselves on *my* back a hundred at a time, but——"

"I know about that," said Bagheera. "I'm sorry Baloo isn't here, but we must do what we can. When that cloud covers the moon, I'll go up there where all the monkeys are. The boy is there."

"Good hunting!" said Kaa. And he moved quickly away to the wall on the far side of the city. That wall was not so badly broken as the other walls, and the big snake lost some time before he found a way over it.

The cloud hid the moon. Mowgli was wondering what would happen next, when he heard Bagheera's quiet feet coming. The Black Panther had run up the hill very fast. Before the monkeys knew he was there, he had started hitting them – it was quicker than biting.

There were loud cries of fear, and the monkeys round Mowgli tried to get away. But then one monkey shouted, "There is only one here!

Kill him! Kill him!"

Fifty or more of the biggest and bravest monkeys threw themselves on Bagheera. They bit, pulled and hit every part of him that they could reach. Mowgli wanted to help him, but five or six big monkeys caught him. They pulled him up the wall of the queens' building. At the top, where there was no roof, they threw him over. He fell five metres to the floor inside. The fall would have hurt other boys badly. But Bagheera had taught Mowgli how to fall, and he landed on his feet.

"Stay there," the monkeys shouted, "until we have killed your friend. Then we will play with you – if the snakes don't kill you."

Mowgli quickly gave the snakes' call. "We are brothers, you and I," he said, with the snake hiss that he had learnt from Baloo. He heard a lot of movement all round him in the old sticks and other things on the floor – snake movement and hissing. So he gave the snakes' call again.

"Yesss, yesss!" said a number of quiet voices. "Stand still, little brother. Your feet could hurt us. Ssstand ssstill." The old building was full of dangerous cobras.

Mowgli stood as quietly as he could. He tried to see through the openings in the walls. He heard the great fight round the Black Panther – the monkeys' shouts and cries, and Bagheera's angry sounds. Mowgli's friend was turning this way and that way, fighting with all his power

Mowgli stands still among the cobras

under a great hill of monkeys. For the first time ever, Bagheera was fighting to stay alive.

"Where's Baloo?" Mowgli wondered. "Bagheera wouldn't come alone." And then he called out: "To the tank, Bagheera! Fight your way to the water tank! Get to the water!"

Bagheera heard him. Mowgli's cry told him that the boy was still alive. And that helped the Black Panther. He fought his way, slowly but surely, towards the water tanks, hitting to one side and the other.

Then, from the wall of the old city, came the roar of an angry bear. Old Baloo had come as fast as he could, but he had only reached the place at that minute.

"Bagheera," he shouted. "I am here! I'm climbing! I'm hurrying! Wait for me. Wait for me, you dirty *Bandar-log*!"

Baloo climbed towards the tanks – and was suddenly hidden up to his head by a great wave of monkeys. He sat back strongly, and began to hit with his great arms – *bat – bat – bat* – throwing dead monkeys to one side and the other.

Mowgli heard the sounds that told him Bagheera had reached the tank, where the monkeys could not follow him. The panther lay there, with his head just out of the water, trying to get his breath back. And the monkeys stood round the tank, a great crowd of them, shouting angrily. They were ready to jump on the panther if he left the tank to go to help Baloo.

It was then that Bagheera gave the snake's call, asking for help: "We are brothers, you and I." He was afraid that Kaa had turned back at the last minute. Even Baloo – under his great wave of fighting monkeys – gave a little laugh when he heard Bagheera asking for help.

Kaa had not turned back. He was coming down the hill – fast, and ready to kill.

The fighting power of a python is in the driving blow that he can give with his head. That blow has all the power of his great body behind it. A python only a metre and a half long can hit a man, and the man will fall down, and you remember that Kaa was ten metres long. His first terrible blow went into the crowd of monkeys round Baloo. His head, with his mouth shut, cut through the crowd. A second blow was not needed. The monkeys that were alive ran away with cries of, "Kaa! It's Kaa! Run! Run!"

For hundreds of years, older monkeys had frightened their young ones with stories of Kaa. "If you aren't good, Kaa will come!" They told their children about Kaa, the terrible night thief: "He can move through the trees without a sound. He can steal away the strongest monkey. Old Kaa can make himself look like part of a tree, and then he can catch even the wisest monkey."

Kaa was the monkeys' one great fear in the jungle. There was no end, they were sure, to his power. No monkey could look into the Rock

Python's eyes. When he turned his body round the biggest and strongest monkey, that was the end.

So the monkeys ran, crying out with fear. They ran to the tops of the old walls. Baloo took a great breath. His skin was much stronger than Bagheera's, but the biting monkeys had hurt him badly.

Then Kaa opened his mouth for the first time. One long hissing sound came from it. The monkeys on the walls and the empty houses stopped their cries. More monkeys, far away in the jungle, were hurrying to help their friends in the monkey city. They stopped when they heard the terrible sound. The city and the jungle round it were suddenly quiet.

Mowgli heard Bagheera climb out of the tank. The noise and cries of the monkeys started again, as they tried to climb higher up the walls.

Bagheera said, "We must take the Man-cub and go. I can't do any more. The *Bandar-log* may come at us again."

"They won't move until I order them to. Ssstay, *Bandar-log!*" Kaa hissed, and the city was quiet again. "I couldn't reach you before, Brother," the great python said. "But I *think* I heard you call, Bagheera."

"Well – yes – perhaps I did call out while I was fighting," Bagheera answered. "Baloo, are you hurt?"

"I think they have pulled me into a hundred

little pieces of bear," Baloo said. "Yes, I am hurt. Kaa, you saved Bagheera and me, and we must thank you."

"I was glad to help. Where is the Man-cub?"

"Here! In a trap. I can't climb out," cried Mowgli.

"Take him away," said the cobras inside. "He is so excited that he can't stand still. He'll hurt our young ones. Take him away."

"Ha!" said Kaa, laughing quietly. "He has friends everywhere, this Man-cub. Stand back, Man-cub. And hide, Cobras. I'm going to break down the wall."

Kaa looked carefully at the wall of the building. A brown line on the white stone showed a place that was not strong. He touched the place two or three times with his head, to be sure to hit it. Then, with two metres of his body in the air, the python gave the side of the building five or six great blows. The wall fell in. Mowgli jumped out through the opening and threw himself between Baloo and Bagheera.

"Are you hurt?" asked Baloo. His voice was kind.

"I am a little hurt, and very hungry. But, oh, my brothers, they have hurt you very badly! I can see you are hurt!"

"Others are hurt, too," said Bagheera, looking round at all the dead monkeys round the tank. "But here is Kaa. He won the fight for us, and he saved your life. Thank him, Mowgli.

Thank him in the way Baloo taught you to say thank you."

Mowgli turned, and saw the great python's head moving from side to side in the air, nearly half a metre over his own head.

"This is the Man-cub, is it?" Kaa said. "He is not *very* unlike the *Bandar-log*. Be careful, Man-cub. You don't want me to mistake you for a monkey one evening."

"We are brothers, you and I," Mowgli answered. "I thank you for saving me tonight. If you are ever hungry when I have killed, the thing I have killed will be yours, Kaa." It was the right thing to say.

"Thank you, little brother," said Kaa. If he was laughing, Mowgli didn't see it. "And what do you kill, brave hunter?"

"I don't kill anything – I am too little. But I drive goats towards those who can use them. And I have these hands: if you are ever in a trap, I may do something with them to thank you – and Bagheera and Baloo. Good hunting to you all."

"Well spoken," said Baloo, because Mowgli had said his thanks very nicely.

"You are brave, little brother," said Kaa, "and you say the right things. But now go away quickly with your friends. Go and sleep, because the moon is going down. It is not good for you to see the things that are going to happen here."

The moon was going down behind the hills.

The lines of frightened monkeys on the walls made no sound. Baloo went down to the tank for a drink. Bagheera began to move away. Then Kaa went with very little sound to the open place between the tanks. His mouth shut with a loud hard sound that made all the monkeys look at him.

"The moon is going down," he said. "Can you still see?"

A sound like the wind in the treetops came from the walls – a sound of fear. "Yes, great Kaa, we can see."

"Good. Now the dance begins – the Night Dance of Kaa. Sit still and see."

He turned a few times round the open place, and then he began to make shapes with his body – O-shapes, 8-shapes, U-shapes, S-shapes – always moving, always changing, never hurrying, never stopping. And all the time a soft singing sound came with the movements.

Baloo and Bagheera stood like stone. Mowgli looked and wondered.

"*Bandar-log,*" came the voice of Kaa at last. "Can you move without an order from me? Ssspeak!"

"Without your order we can't move hand or foot, great Kaa!"

"Good! All of you, come one step towards me."

The lines of monkeys moved one step forward. They could not stop themselves. Baloo and Bagheera moved a step towards the python too.

"Another step!" Kaa hissed. And they all moved again.

Mowgli put his hands on Baloo and Bagheera to make them come away. The two beasts jumped. It was like waking from sleep.

"Keep your hand on me." Bagheera's voice was very quiet. "Keep it on me, or I must go back – must go back to Kaa!"

"It's only old Kaa making shapes on the ground," said Mowgli. "Come away, then." And the three went quietly through an opening in the city walls to the jungle.

"*Whoof!*" said Baloo, when he was under the great trees again. "I won't ask Kaa to help me again."

"He knows things that we don't know," Bagheera said in a voice that was not without fear. "If I had stayed there, I would have walked into his mouth."

"Very many will walk that way before the sun comes up," said Baloo. "He will have good hunting – his way of hunting."

"But what was it all about?" Mowgli wanted to know. He didn't know about a python's power over other beasts. "I only saw a big snake making foolish shapes with his body. And his nose was all broken, Ha, ha!"

"Mowgli," said Bagheera angrily, "his nose was broken for *you*. And it is because of *you*

Kaa dances to the monkeys

that my ears and sides and back, and Baloo's head and body are hurt."

"Yes," said Baloo, "but we have the Man-cub again."

"True. But he has cost us good hunting time, and a hundred bites – and – remember this, Mowgli – I, the Black Panther, needed to call Kaa to save me. All this, Man-cub, was because you talked to the *Bandar-log*."

"It's true," said Mowgli. And he was really sorry. "I am a bad Man-cub, and I am very sad."

"*Hm*! What does the Law of the Jungle say, Baloo?"

Baloo was very unhappy, but he said, "It says: 'Being sorry does not pay for wrong-doing.' But remember, Bagheera, he is very little."

"I will remember. But he has done wrong, and blows must be given. Do you have anything to say, Mowgli?"

"Nothing. I did wrong. Baloo and you are hurt. It is right to hurt me."

Bagheera gave him a few "touches" – but they were a panther's touches, and for a seven-year-old boy they were a real beating. Mowgli stood up, saying nothing.

"Now," said Bagheera, "jump on my back, little brother, and we will go home."

One of the beautiful things about the Law of the Jungle is that a beating is the end of any matter. Nobody says anything about the matter after it.

Tiger!

Now we must go back to the end of the first story, when Mowgli left the wolf cave after the fight at the Council Rock. He went down to the place where men lived, but he didn't stop at the first village. It was too near the jungle, and there were those in the jungle who hated him. So he hurried on, running for thirty kilometres or more without getting tired. At last he was in country that he didn't know.

The open land in front of him had no hills, but it was cut up by ravines. The ravines were dry for most of the year, but when the rains came, the water ran fast along them. So the sides of many of the ravines were like walls. At one end of the open land there was a small village. At the other end, the jungle came to an end near the place where the villagers' cattle and buffaloes found the best grass.

Small boys looked after the cattle and buffaloes there. When they saw Mowgli, the boys ran away. At the village, a crowd came to look at Mowgli. The people talked, and shouted, and pointed at him.

"They are like monkeys," Mowgli thought. "Nobody has taught them." But he opened his mouth and pointed down it to show that he was hungry.

A fat man came. "You needn't be afraid," he said to the crowd. "Look at the marks on his arms and legs. They are the bites of wolves. He is a wolf-child who has run away from the jungle." There certainly were a lot of white marks on Mowgli's brown skin. To Mowgli himself they were not bites: they were places where the cubs' teeth had gone into his skin in play.

"Ah!" some of the women said. "Bitten by wolves? Poor child! He's a nice-looking boy. Messua, he's not unlike your little boy that was taken by the tiger."

A kind-looking woman went over to Mowgli. "Yes," she said. "He does look like my boy."

"Take him to your house, Messua," the fat man said. "Perhaps he is your son. Perhaps he is not. But the jungle took your boy, and the jungle has brought this one back."

The kind-looking woman spoke to Mowgli. He didn't understand her words, but she showed him the way and he followed her. They went into her house, and she gave him milk and bread, and then she put her hand on his head and looked into his eyes.

"Are you my son?" she asked. "Are you Nathoo? Nathoo?"

Mowgli didn't show that he knew the name.

"No," she said sadly. "But you are very like my Nathoo, and you will be my son."

Mowgli looked round the inside of her house. He had never been under a roof before, but he saw that the roof was made of grass. He could break a way through it if he wanted to get away. He understood that this was his new home if he wanted a home among man-people.

"How can I be a man," he asked himself, "if I don't understand man's talk? Now I am as foolish here as a man would be with us in the jungle. I must learn their talk."

Mowgli listened carefully to Messua. As soon as she said a word, he said the sounds of that word. Before night, he had learnt the words for many of the things in the house.

When night came and the door was shut, Mowgli went out through the window. He couldn't sleep in the house: it was like a panther trap. Messua didn't try to stop him. She knew that he had never slept on a bed. Mowgli found some long, clean grass at the side of a field. He lay down there, but he didn't sleep at once. A soft nose touched him. It was Grey Brother, the oldest of Mother Wolf's cubs.

"Pooh!" said Grey Brother. "You smell like a man now. But listen, Little Brother. Shere Khan has gone to hunt far away until his coat grows again. He was badly burned by the Red Flower. But when he comes back, he says, he will put your dead body in the Waingunga River."

"Two can say things like that," said Mowgli. "Remember that I said I will take Shere Khan's skin to the Council Rock. I am tired tonight – very tired with new things. But come again, Grey Brother. Come often, and tell me what is happening in the Seeonee hills and the jungle."

"You will always remember that you are a wolf, Little Brother? Men will not change you?"

"Never. I will always remember that I love you and all in our cave. But I will remember, too, that others made me leave the Pack."

For weeks after that, Mowgli worked hard to learn the words and the ways of men.

In the evenings, he liked to listen to the old men. They sat under a great tree in the village and told stories – wonderful stories. The most wonderful stories were told by old Buldeo, the village hunter. He sat with his old gun on his knees and told wonderful stories about the beasts in the jungle. Mowgli knew that the stories were not true, so he kept his hands over his face to hide his laughing.

But at last the village headman – the fat man – saw Mowgli laughing at Buldeo's story. It was a story about a tiger with one bad foot – the tiger which carried away Messua's son. Buldeo said that it was not a real tiger: it was a ghost – the ghost of a dead giant. "That," said Buldeo, "is why the tiger with the bad foot is afraid of nothing. It is the bravest tiger in India."

"That boy," said the headman, "must have some work. He must go and look after the village cattle and buffaloes. He must take the herds of cattle and buffaloes out to grass in the morning. He must stay with the herds all day. And he must bring them back to the village in the evening. He can start tomorrow."

So the next day, Mowgli went out in the early morning, sitting on the back of Rama, the biggest of the buffaloes and the leader of the herd.

Mowgli was stronger than any of the village boys. He started at once to give orders to the other boys who went out with the herds. "Keep the cattle here," he told them, about a kilometre from the village. "I am taking the buffaloes nearer to the jungle."

At the place where the Waingunga River comes out of the jungle, Mowgli left Rama's back. He ran over to some big trees.

"Ah!" said Grey Brother. "I have waited here for very many days. Shere Khan came back to this country and waited near the village. Now he has gone away to hunt. But he will come back. He wants to kill you."

"Good," said Mowgli. "Will you, or one of your brothers, sit on that rock when he comes back? Then I'll see you when I leave the village."

It was a few weeks later that Mowgli saw Grey Brother on the rock.

"Shere Khan came over the hills last night with Tabaqui," said Grey Brother.

"Oh," said Mowgli. "I'm not afraid of Shere Khan, but if Tabaqui helps him——"

"Tabaqui won't help him. I met Tabaqui this morning. Before I broke his back, he told me everything. Shere Khan is going to wait for you when you go back to the village tonight. He's hiding now in the big dry ravine over there."

"In that ravine?" Mowgli stood and thought. "Has he eaten?"

"Yes."

"The fool!" said Mowgli. "If he has eaten, he can't climb up the sides of the ravine. I can take the herd through the jungle to the head of the ravine. I can make them run along the ravine until they smell the tiger. Then they will be very angry, and they will charge and kill him. But we must stop him from getting out at the other end of the ravine. Grey Brother, can you cut this herd into two parts for me?"

"I can't do it alone, but I have a wise helper."

Grey Brother ran to a hole not far away. A great grey head came up – a grey head that Mowgli knew well, and loved.

"Akela! Akela!" said Mowgli. "How glad I am to see you! Cut the herd into two parts, Akela. Keep the cows and their young ones together, and the bull buffaloes by themselves."

The two wolves ran in and out of the herd, this way and that way. And soon there were two clear herds. The cows were in one herd, with their young ones in the centre. If a wolf stayed still, the cows would charge and kill him with their feet. But Akela and Grey Brother moved

44

The two wolves cut the buffalo herd into two parts

too quickly for that. The bulls looked very dangerous, too.

Mowgli jumped on to Rama's back. "Drive the bulls through the jungle to the head of the ravine, Akela. And you, Grey Brother, keep the cows together. When we have gone, drive them into the other end of the ravine."

"How far?" Grey Brother asked.

"Until the sides are higher than Shere Khan can jump," Mowgli called. "Keep them there until we come down the ravine."

The bulls ran from the great wolf Akela. The cows saw Grey Brother stop just in front of them, and they charged. He ran, just in front of them, to the foot of the ravine, while Akela drove the bulls far round through the jungle.

After a time, Akela stopped frightening the bulls, and Mowgli called quietly to them. It was a long way round, because Mowgli didn't want to take the herd near to the sides of the ravine. Shere Khan must not hear them or smell them.

At last Mowgli stopped the herd at the head of the ravine.

"Give them time to get their breath, Akela," he called. "They haven't smelled him. They need to get their breath. And I want to tell Shere Khan that we are coming. We have him in the trap."

He put his hands to his mouth and shouted down the ravine. The sides of the ravine carried his voice down from rock to rock.

After a long time, the angry voice of a sleepy tiger came back: "Who is it?"

"It's Mowgli. It's time for you to come to the Council Rock, cattle thief! – Now! Hurry them down, Akela! Down, Rama, down!"

Akela gave the terrible full hunting call of the wolf, and the herd started. The bull buffaloes ran into the ravine, going faster and faster. In the ravine, Rama smelled Shere Khan and gave a great bellow.

"Ha!" shouted Mowgli on his back. "Ha! Now you know!" And the herd knew. They knew what they must do. It was the terrible charge of the buffalo herd. Nothing can stop it. No tiger can meet it.

Shere Khan heard the sound of their charge coming down the ravine. He started to move away, looking to one side of the ravine and then to the other for a way out. But the sides of the ravine were like walls. He ran on. The bellow of the charging bulls was answered by a bellow from the cows at the end of the ravine. Shere Khan turned.

Rama's feet hit something – something soft!

Then the charging bulls met the other herd. For a time there was a dangerous sea of buffaloes. But, with the help of Akela and Grey Brother, Mowgli took them out of the ravine, and the buffaloes slowly became quieter.

Shere Khan was dead.

"Brothers," Mowgli said, "that was a dog's end, not right for one of the Hunting People. But Shere Khan was not one of us. He was not brave. He would never have fought." He went with the two wolves to Shere Khan's dead body. "I must take his skin to the Council Rock," he said. "Will you help me?"

With the knife that he carried, now that he was a "man", he started to cut off the tiger's skin. It was hard work. The two wolves helped, pulling the skin the way he ordered.

After an hour, the skin was nearly off. A hand touched Mowgli's shoulder, and he looked up. It was Buldeo with his gun. The other boys had told the village about the buffalo charge, and Buldeo had come out. He was angry because Mowgli had not looked after the buffaloes well. The wolves had hidden when they saw the man.

"What are you doing?" Buldeo said angrily. "Do you think you can take off a tiger's skin? Where did the buffaloes kill him? It's the tiger with one bad foot, too. The Government will give me one hundred rupees for his skin. Leave the skin alone, and perhaps I will give you one of the rupees." He started to pull Mowgli away from the body of Shere Khan.

"Akela," said Mowgli, "the old man is troubling me."

Buldeo suddenly found himself lying on the grass, with a great grey wolf standing over him.

Mowgli cuts off Shere Khan's skin

He lay still. "This is not a boy," he thought. "He is a magician!"

At last, in a frightened voice, the old man said, "Great King! May I get up and go away? Or will your ghost-wolf kill me?"

"Go – without fear. But never trouble me in my hunting again. I have wanted to kill this tiger with the bad foot for a long time. The old man may go, Akela."

Buldeo hurried away to the village, but he looked back often, afraid that Mowgli would change into something terrible. When he got to the village, he told a frightening story of magic and the magician Mowgli, who gave orders to ghost-wolves.

Mowgli finished his work. It was evening when he and the wolves pulled the great skin off Shere Khan's body.

"Now I must hide this skin and take the buffaloes home. Help me to herd them, brothers."

It was nearly dark when they reached the first houses of the village. Mowgli saw lights and heard bells and other noises. "They are glad because I have killed Shere Khan," he thought. But suddenly a lot of stones flew past his ears, and the villagers shouted, "Wolf-child! Jungle-ghost! Bad magician! Go away! Go away quickly! Shoot, Buldeo, shoot!"

The hunter's old gun made a loud *bang*, and a young buffalo bellowed as the shot hit it.

"More magic!" shouted the villagers. "He

can make shots turn away from him. That was *your* buffalo, Buldeo."

"Now what is this?" said Mowgli, as more stones flew towards him.

"They are not unlike the Pack, these brothers of yours," said Akela quietly. "If shots and stones mean anything, I think they want you to go."

"Again? Last time it was because I was a man. This time it is because I am a wolf."

A woman – it was Messua – ran across to the herd. "Oh, my son, my son! They say that you are a terrible magician – that you can change yourself into any beast. I don't think it's true, but go away, or they'll kill you. They are very frightened. Buldeo says you do bad magic, but I know that you have killed the tiger that took Nathoo."

"Come back, Messua!" the crowd shouted. "Come back, or you too will be killed by the stones."

Mowgli laughed – a short ugly laugh, because a stone had hit him in the mouth. "Run back, Messua," he said. "I am not a magician. This is one of the foolish stories that they tell under the big tree in the evening. But I have paid the tiger for what he did to your son. Goodbye, Messua. Now run quickly, because I am going to send the herd in faster than they can throw their stones. Goodbye!"

The buffaloes certainly wanted to get to the village. The noise Akela and Grey Brother made was not really needed. The herd charged into the village like a wave, and the crowd ran right and left.

"Count your buffaloes!" Mowgli shouted. "Count them carefully. Perhaps I have stolen one. Goodbye, Men. You won't see me again."

He turned and walked away, with Akela and Grey Brother beside him. He looked up at the stars, and was happy. "No more sleeping in traps for me, brothers," he said. "We'll get Shere Khan's skin and go away. We won't hurt the village, because Messua was kind to me."

When the moon came up after some time, the frightened villagers saw Mowgli, with two wolves beside him and carrying something big on his head. They were going at the wolf run that eats up the kilometres. Then the villagers made an even greater noise. And Messua cried. And Buldeo told the story of what happened to him, until he ended by saying that Akela stood up on his back legs and talked like a man.

The moon was just going down when Mowgli and the two wolves reached the hill of the Council Rock. They stopped at Mother Wolf's cave.

"They have thrown me out of the Man Pack, Mother," shouted Mowgli. "But I have brought the skin of Shere Khan because I said I would do that."

Mother Wolf walked slowly – her legs were getting old – to the mouth of the cave. Her eyes were glad when she saw the skin.

"I told him that day, when he pushed his head and shoulders into this cave – when he was hunting you, Little Frog – I told him that in the end *you* would hunt *him*. You have done well."

"Yes," said a well-loved voice, "you have done well. How glad I am that you have come back to us in the jungle." And Bagheera came running to Mowgli and the wolves.

They climbed up to the Council Rock together, and Mowgli put the skin over the rock where Akela lay in the old days.

Then Akela lay on Shere Khan's skin and called the old call, "Look well, Wolves! Look well!"

But there was no Pack to hear him.

"Man Pack and Wolf Pack have thrown me out," said Mowgli. "Now I will hunt alone in the jungle."

"Not alone. We will hunt with you," said the four cubs.

So Mowgli went away and hunted with the four cubs in the jungle from that day on.

Questions

Questions on each story

Mowgli's brothers
1 Where was the wolves' cave?
2 What was the tiger's name?
3 What animal is called Tabaqui?
4 How did Shere Khan burn his feet?
5 What was Mother Wolf's name, and what did it mean?
6 What does the name Mowgli mean?
7 Which wolf was the leader of the Seeonee Pack?
8 What does Baloo teach the wolf-cubs?
9 What price did Bagheera pay for Mowgli?
10 What was Mowgli doing while the wolves looked at him?
11 What happened if Mowgli looked hard at a wolf?
12 What was the "Red Flower"?
13 Where did Mowgli get a pot of fire?
14 What did Mowgli do to Shere Khan on the Council Rock?
15 Who did Mowgli go to see before he went down the hill?

Kaa's hunting
1 What words did Mowgli learn for the Hunting People?
2 Which bird's call ended with a high whistle?
3 What was the sound for snakes?
4 Who were the *Bandar-log*?
5 Why didn't Baloo teach Mowgli the Law for the *Bandar-log*?
6 What did Chil the Kite hear?
7 Why did Baloo and Bagheera go to Kaa?
8 How long was Kaa?
9 Who told them where to find Mowgli?
10 When do the Monkey People fight the Hunting People?
11 Where did the monkeys put Mowgli?
12 Where did Mowgli tell Bagheera to go?
13 What does a python use in fighting?
14 How did Kaa break down the wall to free Mowgli?

15 What shapes did Kaa make in his Night Dance?
16 Why didn't the monkeys run away from Kaa?
17 How did Mowgli free his friends from Kaa's dance?
18 What does the Law of the Jungle say about being sorry?
19 How did Mowgli go home?
20 What happens to a wrongdoer in the jungle after a beating?

Tiger!
 1 What cut the ravines through the land?
 2 Who told the villagers that Mowgli was a wolf-child?
 3 What had happened to Messua's son?
 4 Who came from the jungle to tell Mowgli about Shere Khan?
 5 Why did Mowgli hide his face while the old men told stories?
 6 Which buffalo did Mowgli ride on?
 7 What happened to Tabaqui?
 8 Where was Shere Khan hiding?
 9 Who was Grey Brother's wise helper?
10 What did the buffaloes do when they smelled the tiger?
11 Who helped Mowgli to cut off the tiger's skin?
12 Why did Akela push Buldeo over?
13 Why were the villagers frightened?
14 Where did Mowgli put Shere Khan's skin in the end?
15 What is the end of the story?

Questions on the whole book

These are harder questions. Read the Introduction, and think hard about the questions before you answer them. Some of them ask for your opinion, and there is no fixed answer.

1 Many countries have stories about boys or girls who lived with animals. For example, the Romans had a story about Romulus and Remus, who were nursed by a wolf. Do you know any stories of that kind? Could they be true?

2 How did Mowgli learn to speak to
   a animals and birds?
   b people?

3 Baloo:
  a What did Mowgli learn from Baloo?
  b Why did Baloo reach the monkey city *after* Bagheera and Kaa?
  c How did he fight the monkeys?

4 Bagheera:
  a What did he teach Mowgli?
  b How brave was Bagheera? (Give examples.)
  c When was he unkind to Mowgli, and what was the reason?
  d How was he kind to Mowgli
      (i) when Mowgli was a baby?
      (ii) when Mowgli used fire to frighten Shere Khan?
      (iii) when Mowgli came back to the Council Rock?

5 Which animal (or bird, etc.) in this book do you like best? (Give a reason for your answer.)

6 The introduction says that in *The Jungle Book* "the animals are people".
  a Can you give some examples of animals who are "people"?
  b Do you think Kipling was right to make animals behave like people? (Give a reason for your answer.)
  c What kind of *person* was Baloo like? (Give an example.)
  d What kind of *person* was Bagheera like? (Example.)
  e What kind of people are the *Bandar-log* like?

7 Do you like the ending, with Mowgli going away to hunt with the four cubs in the jungle? (Give a reason for your answer.)

New words

bear
a big animal that eats fruit and smaller animals

bellow
(make) the noise of angry buffaloes

buffalo
a big blue-grey, cattle-like, grass-eating animal

bull
the father of young cattle or buffaloes

cattle
cows and their young ones

cave
a big hole in rock or a hillside

charge
run dangerously (with others) towards an enemy; a **charge** is running in that way

deer
a grass-eating animal that runs very fast

fail
not do what one wanted to do

frog
a small green animal without hair; it lives in or near water and can jump well

herd
a number of grass-eating animals of one kind that move and eat together

hunt
run after animals to kill (and eat) them

jungle
forest in a hot country

look after
stay with and take care of

naked
without clothes or fur

pack
a number of animals that hunt together

ravine
a deep narrow cut made in land by a river

roar
(make) the loud noise of an angry tiger

rock
a big piece of stone

shape
the outside look (or feel) of
something

skin
the covering of a body with
(on animals) its hair

snake
a long animal without legs,
sometimes with a
dangerous bite

tank
(in India) a big man-made
place to keep water

tears
water that runs from a
person's eyes

terrible
very frightening

trouble
bad things that happen to
you

village
a small number of houses
for people (**villagers**) who
live together in the country

whistle
(make) a very high sound
like the noise made by air
that is driven through a
very small opening

wise
knowing and
understanding a lot

wolf
an animal of the kind that
cared for Mowgli